Nowhere Lane

Illustrated by
Xareni Ramirez

Written by
Kate Poels

Chapter 1

On the edge of the village where Dexter lived, there was a very unusual lane. It was called Nowhere Lane, because that was where it appeared to lead. Absolutely nowhere.

"Do you think it's actually enchanted?" Dexter's friend, Sam, asked.

They were walking along the lane with its tall hedges in straight rows.

"No," Dexter replied. "It can't be. Can it?"

"I don't know," said Sam. "If we keep going in a straight line then we *should* end up somewhere else, but on Nowhere Lane we can walk and walk and walk and we always end up back where we started."

Dexter nodded. "Maybe it *is* enchanted," he said.

Nowhere Lane was a real mystery to everyone in the village. Lots of very clever people came to investigate the straight road that somehow looped back. They brought expensive equipment that beeped and flashed but none of it helped. Nobody had a good explanation.

Dexter and Sam had been walking in the straightest of lines for almost an hour when, sure enough, they spotted the odd little house on the corner. The very same house they'd walked past on their way into the lane. It had a thatched roof, and the walls, windows, doors and the chimney were all wonky.

Sprat, Dexter's cat, was sitting on the thick bushes outside of the crooked house.

"Don't sit there," Sam said. "Mr Crabtree will come out and turn you into a lizard!"

Dexter's mum had told him not to listen to the other kids when they talked about the old man who lived in the house on the corner of Nowhere Lane. But Dexter knew there was something odd about Mr Crabtree. He didn't come out of his house very often. When he did, he was always scowling and finding things to get cross about.

"Do you really think he could turn Sprat into a lizard?" Dexter asked. "He does look a bit like a wizard."

Dexter was thinking about Mr Crabtree's long grey hair and straggly beard.

"I don't know," said Sam. "But I wouldn't chance it."

Sam had to go home then. It was time for his tea. He waved goodbye and turned left.

Dexter was about to turn right, back to his own house, when a little grey mouse ran out of Nowhere Lane and into Mr Crabtree's garden. Sprat leapt off the wall and sprinted after the mouse, which ran up the side of the house and through an open window. Sprat gave chase, jumping onto the windowsill and squeezing through the little gap. The window crashed shut behind him.

Chapter 2

Dexter tried calling for Sprat but there was no sign of him at all. He kept thinking about wizards and lizards and he started to panic.

"Don't be silly," he said to himself.

Dexter had no choice but to walk up the wonky little path, through the overgrown garden and up to the front door of the house on the corner of Nowhere Lane.

He took a deep breath and knocked on the door. To his surprise, it swung open.

"Hello," Dexter called out. "Mr Crabtree?"

Nobody answered so he called again. He also called for Sprat and hoped that his faithful cat would appear so

they could both get out of there as quickly as possible.

A mewling noise came from down the hallway. It was Sprat. It sounded as though he was in trouble! Dexter knew that Sprat needed him to go inside and help, but he *really* didn't want to bump into Mr Crabtree.

The hallway was dark and creepy, but Dexter crept through the door and tiptoed towards the sound of poor Sprat's mournful meows. On the wall, he saw a picture of Mr Crabtree standing next to a woman. They both looked happy. Not at all like the Mr Crabtree Dexter knew.

At the other end of the hallway was a wooden door painted dark green. It sounded as though Sprat was on the other side of it, so Dexter creaked the door open and stepped inside. He found himself in a dimly lit room full of very odd things... but no Sprat.

There were maps all over the walls. But not like the maps he had seen at school or in the back of his grandpa's car. These maps looked as though they had come out of an ancient story book. Dexter looked at one that was laid out on a table in the middle of the room. He thought he recognised Mr Crabtree's house in the top corner. That meant that Nowhere Lane must be the bright green line that had been drawn next to it. The only thing was that this version of Nowhere Lane *did* lead somewhere. In fact, it led to lots of smaller lanes that all led to other places.

Dexter picked up the map for a closer look. He was sure he felt it crackle in his fingers.

"Hey!" shouted a voice from the door on the other side of the room.

Dexter jumped in shock. It was Mr Crabtree and he looked furious.

Still holding the map, Dexter turned and ran back the way he came. Down the hall and through the front door where he almost tripped over Sprat, who was also making a quick exit.

Chapter 3

Dexter and Sprat ran through the garden with Mr Crabtree thundering along behind them. They dashed out of the gate and Dexter turned towards Nowhere Lane. He noticed Sprat running in the opposite direction, back home, but it was too late for him to follow as Mr Crabtree was getting closer.

Dexter managed to pull ahead when he ran into the lane. Mr Crabtree was not used to running and he was dropping further and further behind, until Dexter realised he couldn't even see him anymore. He must have turned back.

He stopped running and wondered what he should do next. He knew Nowhere Lane well enough to know that whichever way he went, forwards or backwards, he was bound to end up in the same place: right outside Mr Crabtree's house.

Then Dexter remembered the map in his hands. If he was right, then maybe there was more than one way out of Nowhere Lane after all. He stretched the map on the ground and felt another crackle as he smoothed the paper with his hands. Dexter scratched his head. It certainly looked as though there were other paths that led off Nowhere Lane but he had no idea how to find them.

The more he looked at the map, the trickier it was to read. And then something happened that made Dexter stare even harder. The lines started to move and reorganise themselves on the map. It reminded Dexter of when Sprat stood up and turned around before settling himself back to sleep in a different position. But the map was still tricky to understand and not much use, so he folded it up and tucked it into the back pocket of his jeans.

It was then that Dexter spotted something unusual.

On the opposite side of the lane from where he had been sitting, hidden in the leaves and branches of the hedge, was a gate. He had discovered a way out of Nowhere Lane!

Dexter swept the hedge aside and pushed the gate open just enough to squeeze through. When he stepped out, he couldn't believe it. He was right back where he had started, outside Mr Crabtree's house.

At least there was no sign of the grumpy old man. Dexter ran as fast as he could, just in case Mr Crabtree came back. He ran and ran and didn't stop until he was back home.

Mum was in the kitchen cooking tea when Dexter burst through the front door.

"Goodness me!" said Mum. "What's the hurry?"

"Nothing," said Dexter. "Did Sprat make it home?"

Mum looked up. "Who?" she asked.

"Very funny," said Dexter.

Mum rolled her eyes and went back to cooking. Dexter wasn't sure what was up with her, but he could see that Sprat's bed was empty so he left her to it and went to look for his cat. He wasn't in his usual sunny patch on the windowsill and he wasn't in his second favourite spot on the mat by the back door. Dexter decided to check upstairs. No sign of him in the bathroom or the airing cupboard. Perhaps he was lying on Dexter's bed.

When Dexter pushed open the door of his room, he gasped. Everything inside was completely different from how he had left it that morning. His blue walls had been painted green, his rocket ship curtains had been swapped for ones covered in animals, and his giant beanbag had disappeared altogether. But the worst thing of all was his bed. Somebody had come along and taken it away. For some reason they had put a set of bunk beds in its place. His old, familiar duvet was hanging over the side of the top bunk but the bottom bunk was covered by a patchwork quilt made from flowery material. Soft toys covered the bed, including unicorns, bears, frogs, dolls, fairies and even a dragon.

"MUUUUUUM!" Dexter shrieked, pelting downstairs.

Chapter 4

"What's all the fuss?" Mum asked when Dexter rushed into the kitchen.

"What's happened to my room?"

"I tidied it, if that's what you mean," said Mum.

"Who painted my walls green?" Dexter demanded. "Who took away my brilliant rocket curtains and beanbag? And *who* thinks I need bunk beds with flowery covers and a massive load of cuddly toys?"

"Dex, calm down," said Mum. "I'm not in the mood for your silly jokes today."

"*My* silly jokes?" Dexter cried. "I'm not the one making silly jokes. First you pretend you don't know who our cat is and then you change everything in my room and pretend you haven't."

"Dexter, this is all very silly," said Mum. "You know we don't have a cat."

"Then who does that belong to?" Dexter demanded, pointing to the cat bed in the corner of the kitchen.

"That's enough," said Mum. "I have had a long day and I don't want any more of your nonsense."

Mum took four plates from the cupboard and passed them to Dexter. "Dad and Sophie will be back soon so make yourself useful and set the table ready for tea."

"Who's Sophie?" Dexter asked.

At that moment, the front door opened and Dad walked in with a girl who looked around the same age as Dexter. In fact, she looked just like Dexter would have looked if he had been a girl. She was holding one end of a lead. A scruffy little dog was pulling at the other end. As soon as he was unclipped, he ran over to Sprat's bed and flopped down into it.

Dexter stared at the girl.

The girl stuck her tongue out and went over to sit at the kitchen table.

"Mum," she whined. "Dexter is staring at me."

"Right then, twins," Mum said crossly. "I'm telling you now, I'm not in the mood."

TWINS?! What was going on? Dexter didn't even have a sister, let alone a twin. He didn't have a dog, he had a cat. A lovely cat called Sprat who sometimes curled up on his bed with him. His own bed in his own room that had blue walls and rocket ship curtains.

Something freaky was happening and Dexter didn't like it.

He panicked and dropped the plates on the kitchen floor with a huge **SMASH!** And then, before anyone could stop him, he ran out of the front door and away down the road.

Chapter 5

Dexter found himself sitting on a swing in the park. On the surface, everything was as he knew it should be. But the more he looked, the more things he noticed that weren't quite right. The roundabout in the park he knew had been swapped for a row of bouncy cars on giant springs. The slide was blue when Dexter was sure it had always been painted green, and the row of trees that ran down the side of the park looked taller and thinner than the ones he remembered.

Dexter stared at the ground and tried hard not to panic.

"Excuse me. Have you nearly finished?" a lady asked. "My daughter is waiting for her turn."

Dexter looked up and was relieved to see someone familiar. Someone who he knew and who also knew him. It was his teacher.

"Oh," said Dexter, jumping down. "There you go, Mrs Croffy. I was just finishing up."

"Sorry," Mrs Croffy said. "Do I know you?"

"It's me," Dexter said, feeling panicky again. "Dexter Flint. I'm in your class at school."

"I think you've got me muddled up with someone else," said Mrs Croffy. "I'm not a teacher. I work at the post office. Funny though, I did always want to be a teacher before my little Annie came along and my plans changed."

She pointed at the girl, now swinging happily.

What was happening? Dexter needed help and there was only one person he could think of who wouldn't let him down.

It didn't take long for Dexter to run to Sam's house but, when he got there, he paused before knocking on the door. What if Sam didn't know him either? What if he didn't even live there anymore? Sam's mum came to the door and smiled when she saw Dexter.

"Hello, love," she said. "Sam's upstairs. Do you want to head up?"

"Yes please," said Dexter, feeling very relieved.

He took his shoes off and left them at the bottom of the stairs, exactly where he always left them. Then he walked past the same paintings he remembered from the millions of other times he'd walked upstairs to Sam's room.

The rugby poster was on Sam's door, just as it always had been and the music coming from the other side was Sam's favourite band.

Dexter knocked on the door.

"Yeah?" Sam shouted in a silly voice. Typical Sam, always messing about.

"It's me," Dexter said. "Can I come in?"

The door was flung open and Sam stood there, looking as Samish as Sam always did. Sam was Sam in every single way... except for one quite big difference.

This Sam was a girl!

Chapter 6

This was the very last straw for Dexter. He sat down on the floor outside Sam's room and started to cry.

"Dex!" said Sam. "What's happened?"

"Are you really Sam?" Dexter sniffed. "Are you still my best friend?"

"Don't be silly," said Sam. "Why would you need to ask me that?"

"Because you're a girl," Dexter said.

"Duh," said Sam. "That's never bothered you before."

"You weren't a girl before," said Dexter.

"I think you'd better come in and tell me what on earth is going on."

Dexter was very confused but he needed someone to talk to and he recognised his best friend in the girl in front of him. He let Sam help him up and lead him into her room where he sat down on the bed. Sam's bedroom was not *exactly* the same as the one Dexter remembered but it was close enough. He spotted a photograph pinned to her notice board. It was a selfie of Dexter and Sam, identical to the one he remembered taking a few months ago except for the fact that the Sam in this version was the girl he'd just met.

"Well?" Sam asked. "Are you going to tell me what all of this is about?"

"I don't really know how to begin," said Dexter.

The most wonderful thing about a good friend is that they know when they need to trust you. And the most wonderful thing about Sam was that she believed every word Dexter said without a doubt.

"I knew there was something very odd about Nowhere

Lane," she said. "Can you show me the map?"

The map had become a little squashed in Dexter's back pocket but they managed to smooth it out on Sam's carpet.

"Hmmm," she said. "Very interesting. It sounds as though something happened when you went through that gate."

"What do you mean?" asked Dexter.

"I don't know," said Sam. "But I bet Mr Crabtree would."

Dexter shuddered. He had gone through the gate to avoid Mr Crabtree and now it looked as though he might be the only way to get things back to normal.

"But he's so scary," said Dexter. "Isn't there another way?"

"Mr Crabtree?" said Sam. "He's not scary. He's lovely!"

"Really?" said Dexter. It was difficult to believe that the grumpy, fearsome old man in Dexter's world could ever be described as friendly or kind. This new world he had found himself in was getting stranger and stranger all the time.

"I promise," said Sam. "He will definitely help out if he can. Besides, what other choice have you got?"

Chapter 7

The house on the corner of Nowhere Lane was much tidier and brighter than the one Dexter knew. He couldn't believe how he hadn't spotted the difference when he had first run out of the gate and past it. This garden was tidy, with rows of bright flowers instead of clumps of tangled weeds.

When Sam knocked on the door, Dexter still felt nervous—but not for long. Mrs Crabtree answered the door and her smile was so big and kind that Dexter liked her straight away. He recognised her as the woman in the picture that had been hanging in Mr Crabtree's house back in his own world.

"Hello, dears," she said. "How lovely to see you both. Is your mother keeping well Samantha?"

"Yes, thank you Mrs C," said Sam.

"And your family too?" Mrs Crabtree asked. Dexter realised she was talking to him and he nodded.

"We just wondered if Mr Crabtree was home?" asked Sam.

"He is," said Mrs Crabtree. "He's in his workshop at the moment but won't be long. Would you like to come in and have some cookies whilst we wait for him? I've just baked a fresh batch."

The smell was delicious and it only got better as the two friends followed Mrs Crabtree into the kitchen.

Whilst they were tucking into a plate of the best cookies Dexter had ever tasted, Mr Crabtree came in. His hands were stained with ink and he went over to the sink to give them a wash.

"Hello, you two," he said cheerfully.

Dexter could hardly believe it. He could only just tell

that this man was Mr Crabtree. His grey hair was cut short and his beard had been trimmed with a little yellow bow tied neatly into it. But the biggest difference of all was in Mr Crabtree's face. His cheeks were plumper and redder and his eyes sparkled with fun and kindness.

He took a cookie and put most of it in his mouth in one go. Then he winked at Mrs Crabtree.

"My Bess is the best baker in the village, wouldn't you say?" he grinned.

Sam and Dexter nodded and grinned back.

"What can I do for you today?" Mr Crabtree asked.

Dexter took the map from his pocket and laid it out on the table.

"I don't think I belong in this world," he said. "And I hope you can help me to use the map to get back home."

Chapter 8

After Dexter had explained to Mr and Mrs Crabtree what had happened, he thought they would be cross with him for stealing the map. Instead, they seemed sad.

"I don't like the thought of a world out there where I live without my Bess," said Mr Crabtree.

Dexter realised that this must be the reason why the Mr Crabtree in his world was always so grumpy. He was sad and lonely, and he missed his wife.

"Still," said Mr Crabtree, "that is the world you live in and it's my job to get you back there."

"Do we need the map?" Dexter asked.

"We certainly do," said Mr Crabtree. "Come with me and I'll explain how my maps work."

Dexter and Sam followed Mr Crabtree down the hallway. It was much brighter than the one Dexter had crept down to find Sprat because here the curtains had been pushed back and the sunlight was allowed in.

They walked past the picture of Mr and Mrs Crabtree looking happy. Now that Dexter understood what it meant, it made him feel very sad for the Mr Crabtree that lived in his world. Perhaps he could do something to help him when he got back.

"Here we are," said Mr Crabtree, pushing open the door to the map room.

This room was exactly the same as it had been the first time Dexter had seen it. Maps all over the walls and more rolled up in bunches on a big chest of drawers. The table in the middle of the room had a new map set out on it. It looked as though it was only half finished. A pot of pens and a jar of ink stood next to it.

"Did you make this?" Dexter asked.

"I make all the maps," Mr Crabtree said. "I am a cartographer. Just like my mother before me and my grandfather before her. We are a family of map makers that go back many years."

"What do the maps show?" Dexter said.

"They show the paths that link the many different universes together. Universes that run next to ours, but where things are altered."

"So, you're saying I have come through from a different universe?" said Dexter.

"You have," said Mr Crabtree. "And that is not really a very good idea. It is why the gateways stay hidden and why I keep the maps safe. We are meant to stay in our own versions of the world. There will be a Dexter who belongs here and who is now caught in a state of flux."

"What does that mean?" Dexter asked.

"It means he has no world to belong to. He is lost in Nowhere Lane, just walking round and round in loops."

That didn't sound good at all. Dexter knew he would hate that.

"Can you help me and the other Dexter get home?"

"With the map I can," said Mr Crabtree. "It is the key. Without a map, nobody can find the gateways. We have to be absolutely certain we find the right one though, or *who knows* which universe you will end up in."

Dexter laid the map out and Mr Crabtree dotted some ink on to it.

"Put your finger in the middle of the ink," he said.

Dexter did as he was told and the ink began to run. Without Dexter moving, the ink started to draw a new line on the map. It led from the house, through the garden and into Nowhere Lane. A little way down, it stopped and a tiny picture of a gate appeared.

"That's it," said Mr Crabtree. "That's your gateway home."

Chapter 9

The Crabtrees took Dexter and Sam into Nowhere Lane. They followed the inky line on the map until they came to a gate, exactly where the map said it would be.

"Thank you," said Dexter. "It was really nice to meet you."

"Go on now," said Mr Crabtree. "Gates are always shifting around, just like the maps. You need to go through now before this one decides to move on."

Dexter gave Sam a quick hug. "Say hi to the other me when you see him," he said.

"Yeah," Sam replied. "And say hi to the other me when you see *him!*"

Dexter smiled as he pushed the little gate and stepped through, back to his own world. He was right outside the house on the corner of Nowhere Lane and Mr Crabtree was leaning against his garden hedge, waiting for him.

"Find anything interesting in there?" said Mr Crabtree.

"I'm really sorry," Dexter said, handing the map back. "I didn't mean to take it. I just came in to look for my cat and then I saw you and I sort of panicked."

"I thought as much. Well, you're back now so I suppose there was no harm done."

Mr Crabtree turned to go back into his house.

"Mr Crabtree," Dexter called after him.

The old man turned around slowly.

"I met another you behind the gate," Dexter said quickly.

"Oh really?" said Mr Crabtree.

"Yes," said Dexter. "And I met Bess too. I thought she was lovely."

"Well, how about that," said Mr Crabtree, and Dexter could have sworn he noticed a little sparkle in the man's eyes.

"I'd like to help you," Dexter said. "With the maps, I mean. I think it must be a very big job for one person."

"Some days it can be," said Mr Crabtree. He stopped and looked right at Dexter, and nodded his head gently.

"A little help now and then would be mighty fine," he said.

Dexter smiled and Mr Crabtree smiled back, suddenly looking just like the friendly version Dexter had just said goodbye to.

"Have you ever thought about visiting her? Your Bess I mean," Dexter asked. "You could use the maps to go and find her again."

Mr Crabtree looked up at the clouds and scratched his beard.

"Well now, that might be very nice for me. But think about the other me who would end up caught in a state of flux. That would never do, would it?"

"I suppose not," said Dexter.

"You'd better be heading back to that cat of yours," said Mr Crabtree. "But you'd be very welcome to come and help me with the maps whenever your parents say that's okay."

Dexter smiled. "I'll be back very soon," he promised. And it was a promise he knew he would always keep.

Back home, Mum was in the kitchen cooking tea, but Dex didn't stop to chat to her this time.

"Goodness me," she said. "What's the hurry?"

Dexter rushed straight past her and ran up the stairs to his bedroom. Inside he found blue wallpaper, rocket ship curtains, a single bed with his own duvet falling off it, and Sprat curled up in the sun on his giant beanbag. Home, sweet home.

Discussion Points

1. Why does Dexter go into Mr Crabtree's house in the beginning?

2. How does Dexter get into the different world?

a) He reaches the end of Nowhere Lane

b) He travels into the map

c) He goes through a gate on Nowhere Lane

3. What was your favourite part of the story?

4. Who does Dexter meet in the other world?

5. Why do you think the other world's Mr Crabtree was happier?

6. Who was your favourite character and why?

7. There were moments in the story when Dexter had to deal with **change**. Where do you think the story shows this most?

8. What do you think happens after the end of the story?

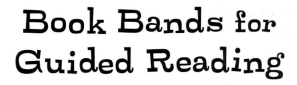

Book Bands for Guided Reading

Pink
Red
Yellow
Blue
Green
Orange
Turquoise
Purple
Gold
White
Lime
Brown
Grey

The Institute of Education book banding system is a scale of colours that reflects the various levels of reading difficulty. The bands are assigned by taking into account the content, the language style, the layout and phonics. Word, phrase and sentence level work is also taken into consideration.

The Maverick Readers Scheme is a bright, attractive range of books covering the pink to grey bands. All of these books have been book banded for guided reading to the industry standard and edited by a leading educational consultant.

To view the whole Maverick Readers scheme, visit our website at

www.maverickearlyreaders.com

Or scan the QR code to view our scheme instantly!

Maverick Chapter Readers

(From Lime to Grey Band)

'Nowhere Lane'
An original concept by Kate Poels
© Kate Poels 2022

Illustrated by Xareni Ramirez

Published by MAVERICK ARTS PUBLISHING LTD
Studio 11, City Business Centre, 6 Brighton Road,
Horsham, West Sussex, RH13 5BB
© Maverick Arts Publishing Limited August 2022
+44 (0)1403 256941

A CIP catalogue record for this book is available at the British Library.

ISBN 978-1-84886-918-9

www.maverickbooks.co.uk

Grey

This book is rated as: Grey Band (Guided Reading)

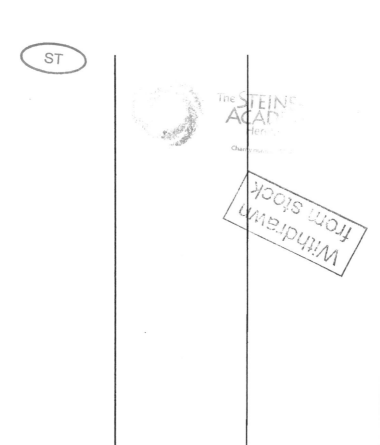